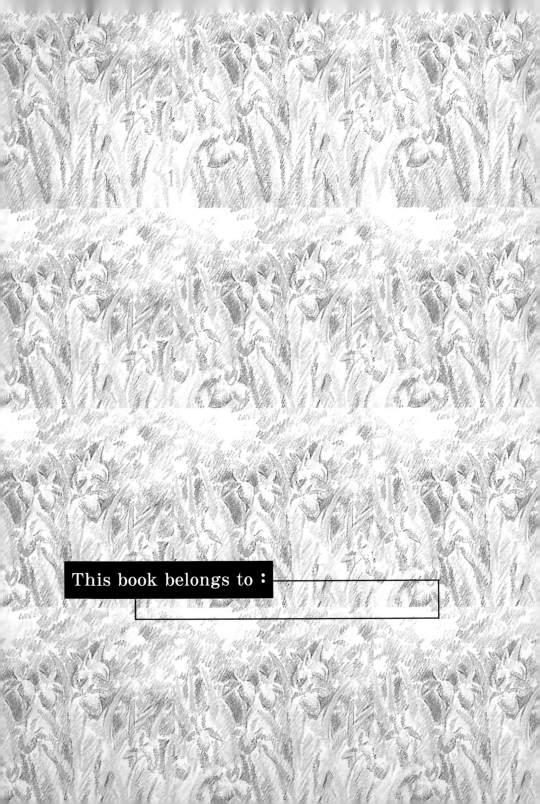

This book belongs to：

The Mysterious Element :
The Story of Marie Curie

Text © Pam Robson 1997
Illustrations © Biz Hull 1997
First published in Great Britain in 1997
by Macdonald Young Books

超級科學家系列
SUPER SCIENTISTS

神祕元素：

居禮夫人的故事

Pam Robson 著

Biz Hull 繪

洪瑞霞 譯

三民書局

Full steam ahead

We're going to **Paris**...
we're going to Paris... the **wheels**
of the train seemed to say,
as they ate up the miles of **track**.
Maria Sklodowska sat **huddled**
on her stool in a fourth class
carriage. She had been on
the train for three days and
Warsaw was now far behind
her. "I'm going to Paris," she
smiled. Paris meant **freedom**!
Freedom to study science.

全速前進

鐵軌飛快地消失在火車輪下，輪子轟隆隆的聲音似乎在說著：我們要去巴黎……我們要去巴黎……。瑪莉亞‧史克羅多斯卡擠坐在四等車廂內，她搭上這班火車已經三天，而華沙也離她愈來愈遠。「我要去巴黎了！」她露出了微笑。巴黎代表著自由，可以盡情研究科學的自由。

Paris [`pærɪs] 名 巴黎（法國的首都）

wheel [hwil] 名 輪子

track [træk] 名 鐵路

huddle [`hʌdl̩] 動 擁擠

carriage [`kærɪdʒ] 名 （鐵路的）客車車廂

Warsaw [`wɔrsɔ] 名 華沙（波蘭的首都）

freedom [`fridəm] 名 自由

Maria **shuffled** uncomfortably. The cold, ladies-only carriage did not have proper seats. Only first-class passengers could travel in comfort; they had coal-fired boxes for warmth. Maria **tucked** her blanket around her cold feet. But her gray eyes **sparkled**.

At last her dream was coming true.

Dawn was breaking as the train **approached** Paris. She **folded** the blanket, pushed a **stray** fair curl beneath her hat and **peered** through the **grimy** windows. At last the train **whooshed** and **gasped** its way beneath the glass roof of the station.

瑪莉亞不舒服地挪動身子。女性專用車廂內冰冰冷冷的，座椅並不高級。頭等車廂內有暖爐可以取暖，也只有那裡的乘客才得以舒服地旅行。瑪莉亞拉起毛毯蓋住冰冷的雙腳，但她灰色的眸子卻閃現著光芒。

她的夢想終於要實現了。

黎明破曉時分，火車就快要駛進巴黎。她摺好毛毯，整理一下帽子底下散亂的鬢髮，從被煤煙燻黑的窗戶向外望去。終於，火車嗚嗚地鳴著汽笛，駛進了玻璃頂罩的火車站。

shuffle [`ʃʌfl] 動 移動
tuck [tʌk] 動 用（毛毯）裏住
sparkle [`spɑrkl] 動 閃閃發光
approach [ə`protʃ] 動 接近
fold [fold] 動 摺疊
stray [stre] 形 散亂的
peer [pɪr] 動 凝視
grimy [`graɪmɪ] 形 被煤煙燻黑的
whoosh [huʃ] 動 發嘶嘶聲
gasp [gæsp] 動 喘氣

Spotted with **soot**, tired and nervous, Maria thought **longingly** of her family in Warsaw. Then she was almost **jerked** off her feet as the train stopped. She **bunched** her skirts and stepped down, a small, **determined** young woman. She had come to Paris to **enrol** as a student of **chemistry** and **physics** at the **Sorbonne** university. Waiting to meet her was her new **brother-in-law**.

疲倦、緊張、再加上一身的火車煤灰，瑪莉亞好想念華沙的家人。火車停穩的瞬間，她便馬上站了起來。這個體型瘦小卻有著無比決心毅力的年輕女子，拉著裙子步下了火車。她來巴黎是為了進索邦大學攻讀物理和化學。來車站接她的是和姊姊新婚不久的姊夫。

spot [spɑt] 動 弄髒
soot [sʊt, sut] 名 煤煙
longingly [ˋlɔŋɪŋlɪ] 副 渴望地
jerk [dʒɝk] 動 急動
bunch [bʌntʃ] 動 收攏
determined [dɪˋtɝmɪnd] 形 堅決的
enrol [ɪnˋrol] 動 註冊
chemistry [ˋkɛmɪstrɪ] 名 化學
physics [ˋfɪzɪks] 名 物理學
[the] Sorbonne [sɔrˋbɑn] 名 索邦大學
（巴黎大學文理學院）
brother-in-law [ˋbrʌðərɪnˏlɔ] 名 姊夫，妹婿

"Maria?" A young gentleman raised his **top hat** and smiled.

"Kazimierz!" The two shook hands. Maria **relaxed**, it was **comforting** to hear a **Polish** voice.

"Are you too tired to walk to the **apartment**?"

"Oh no! I can't wait to see Paris." Maria took her brother-in-law's arm.

「瑪莉亞！」一位年輕的紳士舉起了帽子向她微笑。

「卡基米爾茲！」他們握手寒暄。瑪莉亞鬆了口氣。聽到波蘭口音，令她感到十分安慰。

「看妳這麼累，還有力氣走到公寓嗎？」

「哦！當然可以。我迫不及待要好好地看看巴黎！」

瑪莉亞挽起了姊夫的手臂。

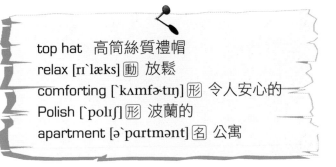

top hat　高筒絲質禮帽
relax [rɪˋlæks] 動 放鬆
comforting [ˋkʌmfətɪŋ] 形 令人安心的
Polish [ˋpolɪʃ] 形 波蘭的
apartment [əˋpɑrtmənt] 名 公寓

Outside, the early autumn sun colored the tree-lined **avenues**. Soon she smelled baking bread and hot coffee. **Wagons** and **carts rumbled** by. Factory workers hurried past. "Here we are, Maria. Our apartment is on the second floor." Sighing with happiness, Maria followed Kazimierz up the stairs.

"I must enrol today," she **announced** firmly at breakfast the next morning. Kazimierz laughed at her **eagerness**. Later that afternoon Maria stood outside the Sorbonne. She watched as students hurried by, talking quickly to each other, and noticed that there were only a few women.

車站外，在初秋的太陽照耀下，綠樹蒼蒼的街道閃著光采。她一下子便聞到剛出爐的麵包及熱咖啡的香味。運貨馬車從身旁轆轆地駛過，工廠工人們也急忙地趕去上工。「到了！瑪莉亞！我們的公寓就在二樓。」瑪莉亞愉快地輕呼了一聲，跟著卡基米爾茲步上樓去。

第二天早上吃早餐的時候，瑪莉亞神情堅定地宣佈：「我今天一定要去註冊！」卡基米爾茲看著她那熱切渴望的神情笑出聲來。當天下午，瑪莉亞站在索邦大學外。她看見學生匆匆忙忙地從身邊走過，彼此迅速地交談著。她也注意到女學生就只有那麼幾個而已。

avenue [ˈævəˌnu] 名 林蔭大道
wagon [ˈwægən] 名 四輪運貨馬車
cart [kɑrt] 名 二輪運貨馬（牛）車
rumble [ˈrʌmbl̩] 動 （車等）轆轆地經過
announce [əˈnaʊns] 動 宣佈
eagerness [ˈigəˌnɪs] 名 熱切

Taking a deep breath, Maria marched through the doors, found the **registrar** and began the business of enrolling at the university. At last, the registrar said, "Please **sign** here," and she wrote her new **French** name, '**Mademoiselle** Marie Sklodowska'.

　　瑪莉亞深吸了一口氣，穿過門，找到了註冊人員，開始辦理註冊手續。終於，註冊人員說：「請在這裡簽名。」她簽上了新取的法文名字：「瑪莉・史克羅多斯卡小姐」。

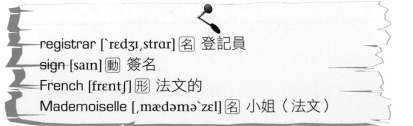

registrar [ˋrɛdʒɪˌstrɑr] 名 登記員
sign [saɪn] 動 簽名
French [frɛntʃ] 形 法文的
Mademoiselle [ˌmædəməˋzɛl] 名 小姐（法文）

Radishes for lunch

Each morning Marie had to make the hour-long **journey** to the Sorbonne on a horse-drawn **omnibus**. But she became tired of all this traveling and after six months she **rented** an **attic** room close to the Sorbonne.

蘿蔔當午餐

　　每天早晨，瑪莉要花上一個小時坐公共馬車到索邦大學上課。她受不了如此疲累的交通往返，於是六個月後，她在索邦大學旁租了一個小閣樓。

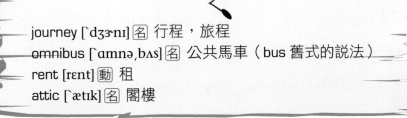

journey [ˋdʒɝnɪ] 名 行程，旅程
omnibus [ˋɑmnəˌbʌs] 名 公共馬車（bus 舊式的說法）
rent [rɛnt] 動 租
attic [ˋætɪk] 名 閣樓

Every day she worked in the half-built science **laboratories**, where the students discussed the very latest scientific **discoveries**. Marie found it much easier to understand French now.

"**Monsieur** Pasteur's work sounds so exciting!" she declared to her friend Jadwiga.

At night, while the male students had fun in the noisy **boulevard** cafés, Marie read alone in her room by the light of an oil lamp. She was too busy studying for her science **degree** to go out and enjoy herself.

每天她都會去尚未完工的科學實驗室做研究。在那裡，學生談論著最新的科學發現。瑪莉覺得法文現在對她來說沒有那麼難懂了。

　　「巴斯德先生的研究聽起來好棒！」她告訴她的朋友加薇佳。

　　晚上，當其他的男學生都去林蔭大道旁喧鬧的咖啡館找樂子時，瑪莉卻獨自在房間裡，點著一盞小油燈，用功地念書。她忙著攻讀理科學位，沒空出去玩樂。

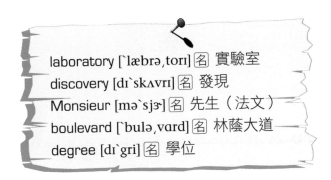

laboratory [`læbrə͵torɪ] 名 實驗室
discovery [dɪ`skʌvrɪ] 名 發現
Monsieur [mə`sjɜ] 名 先生（法文）
boulevard [`bulə͵vɑrd] 名 林蔭大道
degree [dɪ`gri] 名 學位

Her tiny
sixth floor room
had only one window.
In winter it was so cold that the water in her
jug froze. One **freezing** night she **piled** all her
belongings and even a chair on top of the bed
just to keep warm.

她的小房間位於六樓，只有一扇窗。

　　冬天是如此寒冷，連水壺裡的水都結成了冰。有天晚上實在冷得教人發凍，她把自己的所有家當，甚至連椅子都堆上了床，希望能暖和些。

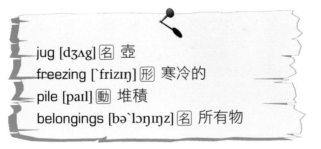

jug [dʒʌg] 名 壺
freezing [`frizɪŋ] 形 寒冷的
pile [paɪl] 動 堆積
belongings [bə`lɔŋɪŋz] 名 所有物

One day when Marie opened her food cupboard, she found nothing there but **radishes**. "Oh well," she **shrugged**, "radishes for lunch." Later that day she **fainted** from hunger. When she told Kazimierz, who was a doctor, he was **horrified**. Marie studied so hard that she often forgot to do everyday things like shopping and eating.

有天，瑪莉打開她存放食物的櫥櫃，發現除了幾顆小蘿蔔外，什麼東西也沒有。「好吧！」她聳聳肩說：「就吃蘿蔔當午飯吧！」後來她餓得昏了過去。卡基米爾茲是個醫生，當瑪莉告訴他這件事時，他嚇壞了。瑪莉念書，用功到像吃飯、出外買東西這種每天該做的事都常會忘記。

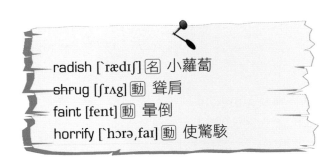

radish [ˋrædɪʃ] 名 小蘿蔔
shrug [ʃrʌg] 動 聳肩
faint [fent] 動 暈倒
horrify [ˋhɔrəˏfaɪ] 動 使驚駭

But all this hard work **paid off**. It took Marie just two years to pass her degree, and she was the top student! She hurried back to **Poland** to visit her family. "We are so proud of you," said her father **delightedly**.

Before long Marie was **awarded** a **scholarship**. This was wonderful — now she would have money to **live on** and the **opportunity** to study again.

So she eagerly returned to Paris.

但這一切的努力都是值得的。瑪莉僅僅花了兩年的時間就拿到學位，並以最優秀的成績畢業。她迫不及待地回到波蘭探望她的家人。「我們真是以妳為榮。」爸爸高興地說。

　　不久之後，瑪莉拿到一筆獎學金。這真是太好了！如此一來她就有錢生活，也有機會繼續攻讀學位了。

　　於是她滿懷希望，很快又回到了巴黎。

pay off　划算，有好結果
Poland [`polənd] 名 波蘭
delightedly [dɪ`laɪtɪdlɪ] 副 高興地
award [ə`wɔrd] 動 授予
scholarship [`skɑlɚˌʃɪp] 名 獎學金
live on　活下去
opportunity [ˌɑpɚ`tjunətɪ] 名 機會

Marie Curie

"**I**f only I had a bigger laboratory to work in," **grumbled** Marie to her Polish friends, the Kowalskis. She **desperately** needed more room for her studies.

"I know someone who might be able to **solve** your problem," said Mr. Kowalski thoughtfully. "His name is Pierre Curie — he works **nearby**."

瑪莉・居禮

「如果我有一間大一點的實驗室就好了！」瑪莉向她的波蘭朋友卡瓦斯基夫婦抱怨。她非常需要大一點的空間來做研究。

「我認識一個人或許可以幫妳解決這個問題。」卡瓦斯基先生想了想說：「他的名字叫皮耶・居禮，就在這附近工作。」

grumble [ˋgrʌmbl] 動 抱怨
desperately [ˋdɛsprɪtlɪ] 副 強烈地
solve [sɑlv] 動 解決
nearby [ˋnɪrˋbaɪ] 副 在附近

Pierre was a science teacher who also loved to study in his **run-down** laboratory. His **invention** of a **sensitive** machine which could **measure** tiny **electric charges** was to be **vital** in Marie's future work.

Although Pierre was only 35 years old, he was already a **respected scientist**. "He looks so young and serious," Marie thought when she first saw him. They spent many hours together talking about science and soon fell in love. They were married in 1895, a year after Marie passed her **mathematics** degree.

皮耶是一位科學老師，他喜歡在自己那間破破爛爛的實驗室中做些研究。他發明一種可以測量微小電荷的高感度機器，對瑪莉後來的研究工作相當重要。

雖然皮耶才三十五歲，但已經是個人人敬重的科學家了。瑪莉第一眼看到他時心想：「他看起來很年輕也很認真」。他們花了很多時間在一起談論科學，不久便墜入愛河！就在瑪莉拿到她的數學學位一年後，他們於一八九五年結婚。

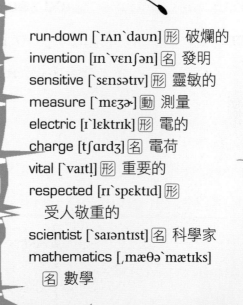

run-down [ˋrʌnˋdaʊn] 形 破爛的
invention [ɪnˋvɛnʃən] 名 發明
sensitive [ˋsɛnsətɪv] 形 靈敏的
measure [ˋmɛʒɚ] 動 測量
electric [ɪˋlɛktrɪk] 形 電的
charge [tʃɑrdʒ] 名 電荷
vital [ˋvaɪtl̩] 形 重要的
respected [rɪˋspɛktɪd] 形
　受人敬重的
scientist [ˋsaɪəntɪst] 名 科學家
mathematics [ˌmæθəˋmætɪks]
　名 數學

Radioactivity

"**P**ierre, Monsieur Becquerel has discovered something odd about **uranium**. He **claims** that it **gives off rays** powerful enough to leave marks on **photographic** plates!" announced Marie.

Pierre wrinkled his brow. "How could that be?" he said thoughtfully.

放射性

　　「皮耶，貝克勒先生發現鈾有一種奇怪的特質。他說鈾能釋放射線，強度足以在照相板上留下痕跡！」瑪莉說。

　　皮耶皺起眉頭，一邊思考一邊說：「怎麼會這樣？」

uranium [ju`renɪəm] 名 鈾

claim [klem] 動 主張

give off 發出

ray [re] 名 射線

photographic [,fotə`græfɪk] 形 照相用的，照相的

Quite by **accident**, Henri Becquerel had found that uranium gave off **mysterious invisible** rays. He had actually discovered what is now known as **radioactivity**.

Marie couldn't stop thinking about Becquerel's rays — there was a **mystery** here that she wanted to solve. She thought carefully about what she already knew.

在很偶然的狀況下，亨利‧貝克勒發現鈾會釋放出一種看不見的神祕放射線。事實上他發現的就是現今所謂的輻射能。

瑪莉不斷地思考貝克勒所發現的放射線──她一心想要解開這個謎團。她仔細地回想自己的所學所知。

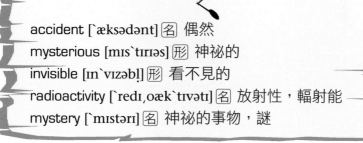

accident [ˋæksədənt] 名 偶然
mysterious [mɪsˋtɪrɪəs] 形 神祕的
invisible [ɪnˋvɪzəbl̩] 形 看不見的
radioactivity [ˋredɪˌoækˋtɪvətɪ] 名 放射性，輻射能
mystery [ˋmɪstərɪ] 名 神祕的事物，謎

Her science studies had shown Marie that everything in the world is **made up of** different **substances** called **elements**. **Iron**, **lead**, **copper** and even **oxygen** are all elements. Most elements are very **stable**; they never change. But **radioactive** elements, such as uranium, are very unstable. When uranium grows older, it gives off tiny radioactive **particles** and very, very slowly changes into lead.

The Curies were not rich and although they loved to study, they had to earn money to live. So Marie trained to become a teacher at a girls' school.

瑪莉所作的科學研究告訴她，世界上每一種東西都是由不同的物質所構成，這種物質就叫做元素。鐵、鉛、銅、甚至氧，都是元素。大多數元素都很穩定，不會起變化。但是像鈾這種放射性元素，就非常不穩定了。在鈾元素的衰減過程中，會釋放出微小的放射性粒子，並以十分緩慢的速率轉化成鉛。

　　居禮夫婦並不富有，雖然他們熱愛研究，卻也必須賺錢生活。所以瑪莉接受訓練成為一名女子學校的老師。

make up (of)　由…構成
substance [`sʌbstəns] 名 物質
element [`ɛləmənt] 名 元素
iron [`aɪən] 名 鐵
lead [lɛd] 名 鉛
copper [`kɑpə] 名 銅
oxygen [`ɑksədʒən] 名 氧
stable [`stebl̩] 形 穩定的
radioactive [ˌredɪoˈæktɪv] 形
　　放射性的
particle [`pɑrtɪkl̩] 名 粒子

Then she found that she **was expecting a baby** and in the autumn, Irene was born.

However, Marie continued to study. She **longed** to become a doctor of science, but to **achieve** that she must study a **subject** that no one had ever looked at before. And she knew exactly what to choose — Becquerel's rays!

"I am determined to find the answer to this **puzzle**!" she **declared**.

然後她發現自己懷孕了，秋天的時候，寶寶愛琳誕生了。

不過，瑪莉還是繼續她的研究。她渴望拿到理科博士學位。但要達到這個目標，她必須找一個沒有人研究過的主題才行。她很清楚地知道自己要選的主題是什麼——就是貝克勒發現的放射線。

「我一定要解開這個謎團！」她鄭重地說。

expect [ɪk`spɛkt] 動 期待
be expecting a baby　懷孕，待產
long [lɔŋ] 動 渴望
achieve [ə`tʃiv] 動 達到
subject [`sʌbdʒɪkt] 名 主題
puzzle [`pʌzl̩] 名 謎，難題
declare [dɪ`klɛr] 動 宣告

So, in a freezing cold, **ramshackle** laboratory, with only a few wooden **worktables** and a **rickety** chair, Marie and Pierre began to **search** for the truth about the mysterious rays.

"I will test other substances," Marie decided. "Perhaps uranium is not the only element to produce these rays of **energy**."

在這間冰冷破舊的實驗室裡，只有幾張木頭桌子和搖晃的椅子，瑪莉和皮耶就在這裡開始研究那神秘的放射線。

　　「我得測試其它的物質，」瑪莉決定這麼做。「也許鈾並不是唯一能釋放出能量射線的元素。」

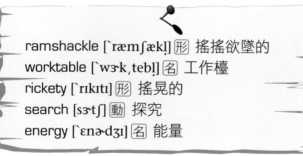

ramshackle [ˋræmˌʃækl] 形 搖搖欲墜的
worktable [ˋwɝkˌtebl] 名 工作檯
rickety [ˋrɪkɪtɪ] 形 搖晃的
search [sɝtʃ] 動 探究
energy [ˋɛnɚdʒɪ] 名 能量

Using Pierre's Piezoelectric **Quartz Balance**, she could work out how much energy different elements gave off. First she tested uranium and measured the strong rays that it gave off. Next she tested **thorium** and found

that it gave off stronger rays. Then she decided to test **pitchblende**.

用皮耶發明的石英電壓平衡儀,她可以測出不同元素釋放能量的多寡。她先測試鈾,並測量它所釋出的強力射線。接著她測試釷元素,發現它釋出的射線比鈾還強。最後她決定測試瀝青鈾礦。

quartz [kwɔrts] 名 石英
balance [ˋbæləns] 名 天平,平衡儀
thorium [ˋθorɪəm] 名 釷
pitchblende [ˋpɪtʃ,blɛnd] 名 瀝青鈾礦

Pitchblende is a mineral which contains uranium. To her surprise, Marie found that it produced much stronger rays than uranium. She was puzzled. The only explanation could be that pitchblende contained another energy-producing element apart from uranium. But what could it be? It must be a completely new element!

"We must find out what it is," said Marie and got ready for some hard work.

瀝青鈾礦是一種含鈾的礦物。出乎意料之外，瑪莉發現這種礦物放出的射線竟然比鈾元素還強。她感到相當困惑。唯一可能的解釋就是，瀝青鈾礦裡除了含有鈾元素外，應該還包含了另一種會釋放能量的元素。但會是那一種元素呢？

一定是還沒被人發現的新元素！「我們一定要找出這種元素。」瑪莉說著。她準備好迎接這個高難度的工作。

Steaming cauldrons

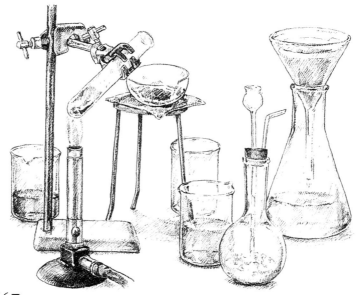

"**L**et's try breaking down the pitchblende with **chemicals**," said Marie. But the results were **disappointing**.

"Why not try **distilling** it?" suggested Gustave Bémont, another scientist. This time the results were better. Even stronger rays were produced. "I think there are two new elements here!" Marie gasped.

鍋鼎沸騰

「我們試試看用化學物質來分解瀝青鈾礦吧！」瑪莉說。但結果卻令人失望。

另一個科學家古斯塔夫・貝蒙建議：「為什麼不試著蒸餾它呢？」這次結果較佳。它釋出了更強的放射線。「我想這裡面應該有兩種新的元素！」瑪莉深吸了一口氣說。

chemical [`kɛmɪkl̩] 名 化學物質
disappointing [ˌdɪsə`pɔɪntɪŋ] 形 令人失望的
distill [dɪ`stɪl] 動 蒸餾

A few months later they were able to **name** one of them. "I think we should call it **polonium**," Marie declared, "after my country."

That summer Marie and Pierre reported that polonium gave off rays which were four hundred times stronger than uranium.

The rays showed that uranium, thorium and polonium were all radioactive.

幾個月後，他們找到其中一種並為它命名。「我想我們應該把它取名為釙，以紀念我的國家波蘭。」瑪莉說。

那年夏天，瑪莉和皮耶發表論文指出，釙元素可以釋出比鈾強四百倍的放射線。

由它們釋出的射線，我們知道鈾、釷和釙都是放射性元素。

name [nem] 動 命名
polonium [pə`lonɪəm] 名 釙

One morning a letter arrived for Pierre. "Marie, listen to this! You've been awarded the **Prix** Gegner. You're to receive 3800 **francs**!"

Marie smiled to herself — important letters were usually sent to a woman's husband, even when they **concerned** the woman herself. "Do you think they will write and tell *me*?" she **joked**.

有天早晨，郵差送來了一封給皮耶的信。「瑪莉！聽聽這個消息！你得到蓋氏獎了！獎金有三千八百法郎呢！」

瑪莉心下暗笑——當時重要的信函通常都會先寄給先生，即使他們要通知的是妻子本人。

「你想他們會親自寫信通知我嗎？」她開玩笑地說。

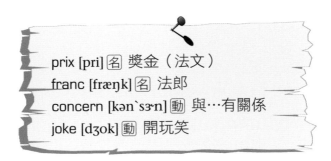

prix [pri] 名 獎金（法文）
franc [fræŋk] 名 法郎
concern [kən`sɜn] 動 與…有關係
joke [dʒok] 動 開玩笑

They still had to **separate** the new elements from the rest of the pitchblende. But for the next three months it was the holidays and time to take a break.

By the end of November Marie was finally able to say **triumphantly**, "There *is* another new element, look at this reading! Its rays are the strongest I've ever seen — they are nine hundred times stronger than uranium! "She wrote in her notebook the name '**radium**'.

雖然找到了釙元素，他們還是必須從剩下的瀝青鈾礦中分離出另一種新元素。但是接下來的三個月，他們決定休息一下，好好地度個假。

　　到了十一月底，瑪莉終於可以很得意地說：「這裡面的確是還有另一種新元素。看這個讀數！它釋出的放射線是我見過最強的——比鈾還強九百倍呢！」她在筆記簿上寫下這個新元素的名字「鐳」。

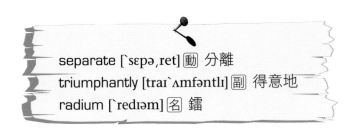

separate [ˋsɛpəˏret] 動 分離
triumphantly [traɪˋʌmfəntlɪ] 副 得意地
radium [ˋredɪəm] 名 鐳

The following spring she **took on** the **enormous** task of separating radium from pitchblende. Pierre turned his **attention** to finding out more about the mysterious rays of energy. They decided to give the strange energy a name — radioactivity.

次年春天，瑪莉開始了艱鉅的工作，試著把鐳從瀝青鈾礦中分離出來。皮耶則把注意力轉移，希望能多瞭解那些會釋出能量的神祕射線。他們決定為這種奇怪的能量取個名字——輻射能。

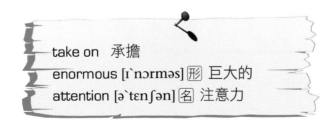

take on　承擔
enormous [ɪˋnɔrməs] 形 巨大的
attention [əˋtɛnʃən] 名 注意力

Sacks containing tonnes of pitchblende — brown dust mixed with pine needles — had been delivered all the way from a country called **Bohemia**.

Now they needed an even bigger laboratory for their work. Pierre and Marie chose a large **shed** with a **leaking**, glass roof, worn pine tables, a blackboard and an old **cast-iron stove**. "At least we can make some tea when the weather is cold," she declared.

For hour after hour, Marie **stirred** huge **cauldrons** full of hot pitchblende with an iron bar almost as big as herself. The **liquids** that she made filled dozens of small **containers**.

一包包的麻袋裝著數公噸重的瀝青鈾礦——混著松葉的褐色土石——它們都是大老遠從波希米亞運過來的。

為了要分解鐳，他們現在需要一間更大的實驗室。皮耶和瑪莉挑了一間很大的儲藏室，有著破漏的玻璃屋頂，幾張破舊的松木桌，一塊黑板，還有一個舊的鑄鐵爐。「至少天氣冷的時候，我們可以在這兒煮壺熱茶。」瑪莉說。

時間一小時一小時的過去，瑪莉用幾乎和她一樣高的鐵棍攪動著一鍋鍋熾熱的瀝青鈾礦。融化的液體裝滿了數十個小容器。

sack [sæk] 名 粗布袋

Bohemia [boˋhimɪə] 名 波希米亞（捷克西部地區）

shed [ʃɛd] 名 倉庫

leak [lik] 動 漏水

cast-iron [ˋkæstˋaɪɚn] 形 鑄鐵的

stove [stov] 名 火爐

stir [stɝ] 動 攪拌

cauldron [ˋkɔldrən] 名 大鍋 [= caldron]

liquid [ˋlɪkwɪd] 名 液體

container [kənˋtenɚ] 名 容器

The glow of success

"I *will* do it," she declared **grimly**. "I *know* there's radium in this pitchblende." She **coughed** loudly. "I do wish the air wasn't always so full of dust, though. But we will find our new elements." She loved the **challenge** facing her.

成功的光環

　　「我一定會成功的！」瑪莉意志堅定地說：「我知道瀝青鈾礦裡一定有鐳。」她大聲地咳嗽著說：「不過我真希望這裡的空氣不要有這麼多塵埃，但無論如何，我們一定會找到這個新元素的。」她喜歡眼前的挑戰。

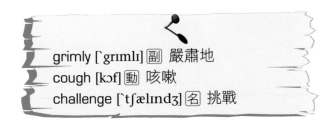

grimly [ˋgrɪmlɪ] 副 嚴肅地
cough [kɔf] 動 咳嗽
challenge [ˋtʃælɪndʒ] 名 挑戰

Although she was deeply **involved** in her **research** into radium, Marie also enjoyed teaching. She was well liked and her students always waited at the classroom window to see their **favorite** teacher arrive. Then they would rush to their seats, ready for an exciting lesson for Marie was able to make science as **fascinating** to them as it was to her.

雖然瑪莉埋首於鐳元素的研究，但是也十分喜歡教書。學生們都很喜歡她，總是等在教室窗口看著她們最喜歡的老師走進來，然後迅速地回到座位準備上這精彩的一課。瑪莉就是能讓學生感受到科學的魅力，就好像科學對她的那種魅力一樣。

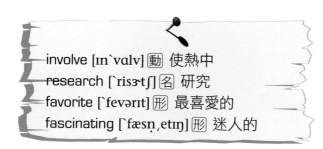

involve [ɪn`vɑlv] 動 使熱中
research [`risɝtʃ] 名 研究
favorite [`fevərɪt] 形 最喜愛的
fascinating [`fæsn͵etɪŋ] 形 迷人的

One warm summer's evening, Pierre and Marie made an **astonishing** discovery. As they visited their laboratory, the **creaky** door **swung** open. **Spellbound**, they gazed at the mysterious **glow** before them.

A strange blue light shone from the glass containers of liquid. "You hoped there might be color in our new elements, Pierre !" Marie exclaimed. Never in their wildest dreams had they imagined that their discovery would **give out** its own light.

They were now close to **success**, but Marie and Pierre were both beginning to feel **unwell**. Marie was losing weight. "I feel so tired," she **complained**, "but I cannot rest when there is so much to do."

Marie and Pierre did not realize how dangerous the rays could be. Radium was beautiful, but it was also a powerful and **deadly** new element.

一個溫暖的夏夜，皮耶和瑪莉有了驚人的發現。當他們走到實驗室，實驗室的門嘰嘰嘎嘎地晃了開來。像著了魔似的，他們凝神望著眼前的神祕亮光。

　　一道奇怪的藍光從裝了液體的玻璃容器中射了出來。「皮耶！你不是希望我們的新元素會有顏色嗎？」瑪莉興奮地說。他們做夢也想不到他們發現的元素能射出自己的光芒。

astonishing [ə`stɑnɪʃɪŋ] 形 令人吃驚的
creaky [`krikɪ] 形 嘰嘰嘎嘎響的
swing [swɪŋ] 動 搖晃
spellbound [`spɛl͵baund] 形 被魔法鎮住的
glow [glo] 名 光
give out 發出

他們離成功不遠了，但瑪莉和皮耶卻開始感到身體不適。瑪莉變得愈來愈瘦。「我覺得好累啊！」她抱怨地說：「但我不能休息，還有好多事要做呢！」

　　瑪莉和皮耶並不知道這些放射線有多麼危險。鐳很漂亮，但它也是一種強力的、致命的新元素。

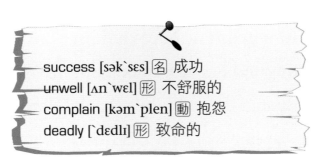

success [sək`sɛs] 名 成功
unwell [ʌn`wɛl] 形 不舒服的
complain [kəm`plen] 動 抱怨
deadly [`dɛdlɪ] 形 致命的

The Nobel Prize

Then at last came the day the Curies had been working **toward**. As Marie held up a tiny container, she knew this was it! The result of all their hard work was one-tenth of a **gram** of pure radium.

Marie invited her students from Sevres and her sister Bronia to watch her receive her **doctorate** for her work on Becquerel's rays. Marie had to answer questions on her amazing research and on the discovery of the two new elements: radium and polonium.

諾貝爾獎

　　終於，居禮夫婦達成了他們一直在努力的目標。瑪莉舉起手上的小瓶子，她知道這就是了。他們辛苦工作的成果就是這 0.1 公克的純鐳元素。

　　瑪莉以她對貝克勒放射線研究的成果，拿到博士學位。她邀請姊姊布蘭尼雅和她在塞佛爾的學生到場觀禮。對於她驚人的研究及發現釙和鐳這兩種新元素，瑪莉必須回答大家對此所提出的問題。

toward [tord] 介 朝向…
gram [græm] 名 公克
doctorate [`dɑktərɪt] 名 博士學位

"Isn't Madame wonderful!" the students sighed, amazed and delighted to see a woman achieve success in the world of science. That night, in a friend's garden, Pierre proudly **demonstrated** the glow from a tube of their radium. It was a wonderful end to the day.

「老師真是太棒了！不是嗎？」學生們驚嘆地說。他們對於一個女人能在科學的領域裡有這麼大的成就感到驚訝，同時也相當高興。當天晚上，在朋友的花園裡，皮耶拿著試管，驕傲地向大家展示鐳所發出來的光，為這一天寫下完美的句點。

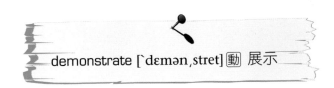

demonstrate [ˋdɛmənˌstret] 動 展示

At the end of 1903, the Curies and Henri Becquerel were awarded the Nobel Prize. But some newspapers claimed, "Madame Curie only helped her husband in his work." They were unwilling to believe that a woman could be a scientist.

西元一九〇三年底，居禮夫婦及亨利‧貝克勒一起獲得諾貝爾獎。但有些報紙卻報導說：「居禮夫人只是從旁協助她的先生而已。」他們不願意相信，一個女人也能成為科學家。

Though they had achieved worldwide fame, the Curies remained **dedicated** to their research. Pierre had to write to the **Swedish Academy**, "We will be unable to **attend** the award **ceremony**. Madame Curie is unwell, and we cannot take time off from our work." This simple **modesty** was **typical** of them. "Radium does not belong to us," they insisted, "it is for the world."

雖然居禮夫婦已經舉世聞名，但他們仍致力於研究。皮耶不得不寫信給瑞典學院：「我們無法前去參加頒獎典禮。居禮夫人身體不適，而我們的研究工作又很忙，實在無法抽身前往。」這就是他們一貫的謙虛態度。「鐳並不屬於我們，它屬於全世界。」他們強調。

dedicated [ˈdɛdə͵ketɪd] 形 熱中的
Swedish [ˈswidɪʃ] 形 瑞典的
academy [əˈkædəmɪ] 名 學院，學會
attend [əˈtɛnd] 動 出席
ceremony [ˈsɛrə͵monɪ] 名 儀式
modesty [ˈmɑdəstɪ] 名 謙恭
typical [ˈtɪpɪkl] 形 典型的

Epilogue

On a wet day in Paris, in 1906, Pierre died **tragically**, **knocked** down by a horse-drawn wagon. Marie **overcame** her grief and continued her work alone. Despite her poor health, which was growing worse, she traveled to America and Britain and attended international **conferences**.

後記

　　西元一九〇六年一個陰雨天，皮耶在巴黎被一輛貨運馬車撞倒，不幸死亡。瑪莉強忍住悲傷，獨自繼續她的研究工作。儘管身體不適，病況愈來愈糟，她還是四處奔波，到美國及英國參加國際研討會。

tragically [`trædʒɪklɪ] 副 悲劇性地
knock [nɑk] 動 撞擊
overcome [,ovɚ`kʌm] 動 克服
conference [`kɑnfərəns] 名 會議

Marie Curie's greatest achievements were the discovery of radium and the fact that radioactivity came from the **atom**. Because of her **precise** scientific work, and her determination to succeed, doctors can now **treat** and even **cure cancer**, **archaeologists** can tell the age of ancient objects and **nuclear** power is used to produce **electricity**. Sadly, the discovery has also led to the **destructive** power of nuclear weapons.

In Britain, her name **lives on** in the work of the **charity** Marie Curie Cancer Care, which provides free **nursing** for people with cancer and carries out research into the causes of cancer.

瑪莉‧居禮最大的成就就是發現鐳元素及證實輻射能是由原子而來。現在醫生可以治療甚至治癒癌症，考古學家可以測出古物的年代，核能可以用來發電等，都要歸功於居禮夫人嚴謹的科學研究和堅持到底的決心。但不幸的是，這個發現也導致人類發明了毀滅性的核子武器。

　　在英國，瑪莉‧居禮癌症療養中心是一個免費照顧癌症病人，以及研究癌症病因的慈善機構。瑪莉‧居禮的名字從此長留於人們的記憶中。

atom [ˋætəm] 名 原子
precise [prɪˋsaɪs] 形 精確的
treat [trit] 動 治療
cure [kjʊr] 動 治癒
cancer [ˋkænsɚ] 名 癌
archaeologist [ˌɑrkɪˋɑlədʒɪst] 名 考古學家
nuclear [ˋnjuklɪɚ] 形 核子的
electricity [ɪˌlɛkˋtrɪsətɪ] 名 電力
destructive [dɪˋstrʌktɪv] 形 破壞性的
live on　長存
charity [ˋtʃærətɪ] 名 慈善機構
nursing [ˋnɝsɪŋ] 名 看護

Timeline

Marie Curie was born on 7 November 1867 in Warsaw, Poland.

1891 *Marie leaves Poland and enrols at the Sorbonne University in Paris.*

1895 *Marie marries Pierre Curie.*

1895 *Wilhelm Röntgen discovers X-rays.*

1896 *Henri Becquerel discovers the radioactivity of uranium.*

1897 *The Curies' daughter, Irene, is born.*

1898 *The Curies discover a new element — they name it polonium.*

1899 *Marie begins the task of finding another new element — radium.*

1902 *Marie isolates one decigram of radium.*

1903 *Marie and Pierre Curie and Henri Becquerel win the Nobel Prize for Physics.*

1906 *Pierre Curie is killed in a tragic accident.*

1910 *The standard unit of measurement of radioactivity — the curie — is set up.*

1911   Marie Curie wins the Nobel Prize for Chemistry.

1914   Marie organizes mobile X-ray units during World War One.

1932   Scientists split the atom. The geiger counter is invented to measure radiation.

1934   Irene and Frederic Curie-Joliot discover artificial radioactivity.

1942   The first nuclear reactor is set up in Chicago, USA.

1945   Atomic bombs are dropped on Japan.

1962   Cobalt-60, an artificial radioactive substance, is used to treat cancer.

Marie Curie died on 4 July 1934 in France. She was 66 years old.

生平紀事

一八六七年十一月七日，瑪莉・居禮誕生於波蘭華沙。

1891　瑪莉離開波蘭，就讀於巴黎索邦大學。

1895　瑪莉嫁給皮耶・居禮。

1895　威漢・侖琴發現X射線。

1896　亨利・貝克勒發現鈾的放射性。

1897　女兒愛琳出生。

1898　居禮夫婦發現新元素，取名為釙。

1899　瑪莉試著開始找出另一新元素——鐳。

1902　瑪莉分離出 0.1 公克的鐳。

1903　居禮夫婦和亨利・貝克勒獲頒諾貝爾物理學獎。

1906　皮耶・居禮死於車禍意外。

1910　設定「居里」為輻射能的標準測量單位。

1911　瑪莉・居禮獲頒諾貝爾化學獎。

1914　第一次世界大戰期間，瑪莉成立X射線醫療機動組織。

1932　科學家分裂原子。蓋革計數器被發明用來測量輻射能。

1934　愛琳・居禮和先生佛雷德瑞・居禮——約里歐發現人造輻射能。

1942　第一座核子反應爐在美國芝加哥設立。

1945　美軍在日本廣島投下第一顆原子彈。

1962　人造放射物質——鈷60——被用來治療癌症。

一九三四年七月四日，瑪莉・居禮逝世於法國，享年六十六歲。

atom [ˋætəm] 名 原子

the tiniest particle of an element that can take part in a chemical reaction

cancer [ˋkænsɚ] 名 癌

this disease affects cells in the body — radiation treatment, called radiotherapy, can kill cancer cells

curie [ˋkjʊri] 名 居里（輻射能的測量單位）

the 'curie' is a measure of radioactivity

element [ˋɛləmənt] 名 元素

everything in the world is made up of different mixtures of elements

nuclear physics 核子物理學

the area of science which studies the atom and what is inside it

Piezoelectric Quartz Balance 石英電壓平衡儀

a machine which measures tiny amounts of electricity

radiation [ˌredɪˋeʃən] 名 放射能

energy in the form of rays given out from the atom

radioactivity [ˌredɪˌoækˋtɪvətɪ] 名 放射性，輻射能

when some elements break up and give off radiation

x-rays X 射線

these are used to photograph bones inside our bodies

Vocabulary隨身讀系列

- 口袋型設計易帶易讀，分秒必爭學習最有效率。
- 廣納各階段必考單字，依據使用頻率排列，分級學習最科學。
- 增補重要同反義字與常見片語，助您舉一反三、觸類旁通。

國家圖書館出版品預行編目資料

神秘元素：居禮夫人的故事 =The mysterious element：
the story of Marie Curie ∕ Pam Robson著；Biz Hull繪；
洪瑞霞譯. －－二版二刷. －－臺北市：三民，2014
　　面；　公分. －－(超級科學家系列)

ISBN 978－957－14－2989－2　 (平裝)
1.英國語言─讀本

805.18　　　　　　　　　　　　　　　　8803983

ⓒ　神秘元素：居禮夫人的故事

著 作 人	Pam Robson
繪　　者	Biz Hull
譯　　者	洪瑞霞
發 行 人	劉振強
發 行 所	三民書局股份有限公司
	地址　臺北市復興北路386號
	電話　(02)25006600
	郵撥帳號　0009998－5
門 市 部	(復北店)臺北市復興北路386號
	(重南店)臺北市重慶南路一段61號
出版日期	初版一刷　1999年8月
	二版一刷　2012年9月
	二版二刷　2014年9月
編　　號	S 854870

行政院新聞局登記證局版臺業字第○二○○號

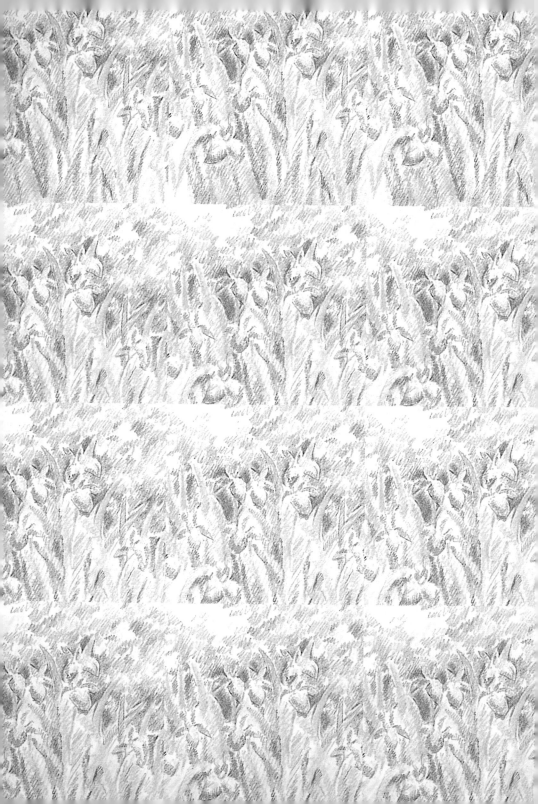